Synchronicity

# Synchronicity

A collection of poems by  Lee JongMin
Translated by  Levi Lee

동시존재  이종민

K-Poet Series 038

ASIA

# Contents

**Reality 1**

| | |
|---|---|
| Synchronicity | 10 |
| Walking Trail | 14 |
| Closed Eyes | 18 |
| Infinite Power | 22 |
| Little Ark | 24 |
| Shining Matter | 28 |
| Dish Filling | 32 |
| I Have Fought the Good Fight | 36 |
| Déjà Vu | 38 |
| I Have Finished the Race | 42 |

**Reality 2**

A Waiting Person                          46

Fractal                                   48

Planned Community                         50

Nude                                      52

Holiday                                   56

Sandwich                                  60

Ellipsis                                  62

The Longing Meadow                        66

I Have Kept the Faith                     70

Summer, Decline and Then Blackout         72


Poet's Note                               77

Poet's Essay                              81

Commentary                                85

Praise for Lee JongMin                    97

# SYNCHRONICITY

**Reality 1**

## Synchronicity

Walking all day with a person who only comes
out in dreams
   I stepped on
   the ground forming above the coordinate plane

   There's no here and there
   Can't distinguish up from down

   That's it for the world I used to know

   Days of washing my heart when it rains
   and waiting for the rainbow

   A gravel road and a green forest

A hand pushing through the water
in a pool
The number on my bank account
and the countless letters printed
on the white plane

Holding a knife
that was talking about conviction and
the hesitation of chopping a finger off along
with the vegetables while
holding a knife

I'll tell you the things you'll have to go through
from now on

The eyes of a person putting their hand on
your shoulder
The rippling past

Some day in the future, I described that
as love's advent

## Walking Trail

We each decided which way to go in front of the milepost.

The path that went downhill

and the path that went uphill.

The expected junction was the octagonal pavilion. He told me that there is a bench in the pavilion, and an old bench press and some mineral water nearby. We each took paper cups, saying that the first person to arrive should get the water. He also told me that we have to line up to get it.

The smell of dried leaves emanates from his

body. The smell is similar to the smell of rotting wood grain.

They say this mountain was originally a cemetery. I walked as I listened to the conversations of others. A path with straight trees, curved trees, and more curved trees shaped in different ways.

I walked for a long time thinking about the word, 'originally'.

Aren't you curious where we'll meet if we walk in opposite directions?

I walked as I ruminated on his words. I walked as I thought about my mind being curious about curious things.

Footprints lined up towards the octagonal pavilion.

Squatting down, I look at the water falling into the paper cup. A sound that's loud enough to muffle anyone's footsteps.

Though the tree is dying

and he doesn't come—in the mountain where he's coming from.

I'm going to keep going—holding two paper cups filled with mineral water.

## Closed Eyes*

The wind that ran into you gathers weight. You close your eyes and fall asleep. Into a dream. Into a dream where only the world you know exists and you don't.

Even in dreams, I know that someone is exhaling. I know that trees are sucking in the earth. I know that rivers are surging with doom.

When you look at the end of the hill or behind you on your walk, your body knows that there is an energy that vanishes. You know that light has been burning you from long ago and you know that the star that arrived in front of your eyes has been hiding millions of years behind its back.

You pretend not to know. Melody of leaf colliding with leaf and explosions of falling raindrops.

The fact that the river is flowing into your eyes, to a place within you that you don't even know.

Peace is barely kept alive behind your back. Exquisitely, so that you can feel it even though you can't see it. The ground spins beneath your feet and everything gets gradually closer as day and night devour each other.

When someone's fingertips touch your shoulder. The moment you turn your head.

The wind blows on doom. The universe without you dreams of the future.

* Odilon Redon, *Les Yeux Clos*, oil on canvas, 44x36 cm, 1890.

## Infinite Power

The road goes by as I step on the pedals. The pedals erase my legs as they spin. Speed sticks onto my hair. The road doesn't allow the end. The end bites onto the road, tenacious.

The speed of water is called a river. A river that's there even when I step on the pedals or hold the brakes. A river that's there even when I'm not.

We are watching the same river before we know it. In the middle of some road. Although we never made a promise.

We pass by even without pedaling. The river looks calm even though the water is fast. We keep by the river despite the speed.

The pedals display trees and cosmoses as they turn. The end displays the end as it passes by. We watch ourselves. We recall ourselves.

I wish I had a name to call this speed. Like a river. Like we're not ourselves beyond the dead end.

We walk over ourselves. Today bites onto today, tenacious. The day is about to overflow.

## Little Ark*

There is more future for a ship on the ground
than a ship on the water

Although more isn't necessarily better

People
like many uncertain things more than a single
certain thing

A bird is flying inside a big birdcage

We grab hands for the first time

Imagining a western house that Young-hee

likes

   in front of a hanok that Smith likes


I think of lyrics like

*Suzanne, dusk is falling*

*Oh, Suzie Q*


For *jeong,*

warmth is more important than quantity


Take it easy, take it easy


I like driving and

although sleep aid gums taste worse

than nicotine gums,

people are more attracted to things that are
moderately uncomfortable


A bird cage whose insides are in full view and

a sculpture that is nice for unexplainable
reasons


We are on the same boat just for a moment

When the water slowly rises, each of our
destinations come into being

Those that we like despite never knowing what
they are

## Shining Matter

At the entrance I find it:
round and quiet like a crouching beast
I leave it as is, assuming someone left it by
mistake

The light comes in all day in the new house
with walls of glass
and the sunlight gives hope for the future

New furniture and appliances come in
Days of passing the corridor and putting the
wrong password in the front door

It's shining on its own

The light stops like a lie when I hug it with
both hands
　but I can't stop sneezing
　Every time I sneeze the seasons fly by


　Because I can feel the light even when I put it
deep into the closet
　I sleep with it in the bed—it's a dark, tranquil
night if I can hug it and endure its memories—
I go to sleep, sneezing,
　and the shining thing crushes me to death
　The light burns me to death
　I'm abruptly put to death

Tending my memory with the sunlight and the lighting

I look at the thing sleeping on the bed—it's cold and shining faintly

Something about it makes me sneeze

One that's powerful enough to reach another world in a heartbeat

Those who left and those who left forever

I decide not to rush

It was a matter of honoring and mourning

## Dish Filling

On a table is an empty dish
A dish reflecting a face
What does an empty dish want to hold?

I put it face down on a dish rack
The face reflected on the dish changes

A person who eats with me says I've changed
When I ask, "From when?"
he looks at my face without a word
The empty dish dries
and that person glares at me with his hair
turned gray
"You don't listen to my words"

Water falls from an empty dish

Red soup goes in the empty dish
White rice goes in the empty dish
and boiled meat goes in the empty dish
People come to see him who doesn't exist
and tell me I haven't changed a bit

The dish seems to be smiling
The empty dish is dripping water

People say
he must have thought of me

I can't recall his old face

and there's still water on the dish—the dish is

slipping

White hair falls

A face reflected on an empty dish

The dish wants to take after it

# I Have Fought the Good Fight*

I walk on as I'm beaten down. My legs rise as I'm beaten up. My body and my head are clear. Names hit me. Coats, hair, and objects hit me. I'm clear. *Touch my skin. My skin is warm.* Hitting me with eyes like that, you're in pain. Pain hits me. Explosions all around. Pain is glaring. Crumbling paths are bright. The world is falling apart—hitting each other, beating each other. It's becoming clearer.

* 2 Timothy 4:7

## Déjà Vu

When should we have lunch?
I was about to ask, but noon passed

In my dream that I dreamed all last night, I
was at the beach, drawing promises to come on
the sand; although I want to remember all the
footprints that we left, the waves rise
  and I surge
  and I become clear

The wind that took you doesn't return from
the other side of the Earth; although you who
has not arrived will be somewhere by the cliff
that soars up every time I step on the ground

and where a storm rages with a single clearing of
one's throat


looking at my toes
I imagine the place that I'll be in a few seconds


When should we have lunch?
There was a time when I fell down at midnight
having such thoughts
Red flowers and red waves
that bloom on my knees
Footprints swept away splash in the water
The horizon changes places with you

The eye of the sea is so big
that it needs an eternity for a single blink

The sky keeps falling
not even knowing that,
and from within,
your toes can be seen now and then

# I Have Finished the Race*

I imagine the hell that you have to go to every day
I believe that it's heaven

Eyes that don't meet another to be transparent
I consider it fate

In front of a wall
I am the dream that you wanted to dream
The single shadow that you had

A question drives a nail on a wall
Pondering what to hang
a lifetime passes

If I close my eyes
a distant memory draws back

Between embarrassment and love
Between countless strolls and humiliation
Between misery and remorse

How much more light can you give me?
Even if that can't burn a clump of grass
an instant is soon an eternity

When I turn my head to face away from the wall
there are a thousand walls again

* 2 Timothy 4:7

**Reality 2**

## A Waiting Person

I'll go down to the entrance on time

If I hang around the entrance,
time tip-taps
past my shoulders

When I count the floors, there is a floor I can't
see
Although people are breathing there too

There's no one here—the person you're looking
for isn't here
The entrance approaches rearranging its hat

The height from the entrance shoots up
From the roof, from the railing, from the
window,
silence pours down

Stairs that stack up on numerous different
times
Leaving cars fill up the streets

I'll wait in front of the door

The elevator opens and people pour out
That person is all over the world

## Fractal

People live even on the other side of the earth
I can't hear them breathing

It feels strange to listen to their recorded voice

That wasn't what I meant,
  but that's what it ends up meaning when I see
their back

  Blood flows when flesh is cut
  Even though veins remain untouched

  A day ends—someday I'll die

I think I've come back a long way
from a place far away

From a place high up, a line of streetlamps
looks like a single light
There are a lot of stars in the sky out of sight

In the dark

I feel my skin
I can hear the sound of breathing

## Planned Community

A lot of things happened and a lot of things didn't. A few people arrived and even more left. They filled the empty space and built on the empty space. Dust that wasn't there before came into being and the dust that wasn't there before will be born. There will be muscle pain and neighbors that don't exist now. Heat absent in winter and warmth absent in sub-zero rise. Sweat forms. They drink water. Water that was there and the water that wasn't. Things that have to be moved are still scattered. Things that are moved pack the space. People that are moving and people that are moved go into their respective floors. Not a few things have happened and not a few things haven't. A few memories of hopes and expectations are stored away. They are haunted by a few regrets and despair.

# Nude

Coats that don't hang neatly on the hangers

Pizza, soup, and seafood become mishmash in
my stomach without even a plate
Breakfast, lunch, and dinner walk together as
one body

Monday is closer Tuesday than 월요일
and 월요일 feels close to 화요일

Round frames that decorate the table when the
time comes
I draw pizza, soup and seafood that was in my
stomach

and close my eyes
May the gods grant an end to this boredom

I count steadily from 1 when I pray
Because 0 is already counted

Hunger is
proof that words desire bodies

Monday tries to change to Tuesday
and 월요일 to 화요일
Even if we stay still

We will be death by tomorrow

Taking off our coats here and there
steadily from 1

Until we reach 0
don't have thoughts that you can't contain

Why are mouths just one?

## Holiday

I drink beer on the riverside. My mouth comes and goes where your mouth rests. When your loosely tied hair shakes in the wind, the world goes somewhere else. Lying next to me on a mat, you talk about your budget for this month and not a single car passes through the bridge built over the river. Your speech is slow and careful like its crossing a stone bridge and the end of your words resonate like lingering echoes over hills.

Even if I chew over the words that you spit out, ten times per sentence, I can't tell where you're heading. Even though it's serene over the bridge and I have a hunch that it will start to drizzle from the smell of water.

This place is in the middle of summer. I was going to say that the etymology of *jeomsim* (lunch) suggests the word has the meaning of soothing hunger, like putting a dot on a heart, but I just say, If I'm rice, you're side dish. If you're rice, I'm side dish. In our dreams, let's talk about what we couldn't tonight. Should we fry sausages in the shape of octopuses tomorrow? Should I tie your shoelaces in the shape of butterflies?

If I follow the grass lying down in the shape of feet, a river emerges and bugs cry nearby, and across the river, will there be grass lying down, wet from the water by the shore?

I wish the sound of rain will flow through the hazy ceiling when I wake up from here. I wish it is chilly. I wish the asphalt is black and wet. Do you also sleep with a fan on all night? Do you dream of flying in the sky with a fan? I hope we dream of flying together at the same time.

Let's do it. You replied even when I hadn't said a word. Let's do it. Then my eyes open from the damp blanket. The pillow is neat without a wrinkle and the sausage in the fridge is long gone. A pair of shoes on the porch. Let's do it,

I think there were some more words that were said

## Sandwich

I think there is something between us. With those words your body appears in front of me. When I whisper, I love you, I love you, I love you, you become a piece of meat. I think of everything there is to about meat. The more I bite off a thought the harder flesh becomes. The floor, the ceiling, the wall, your face permeates them all. Then you disappear. A thought is fragrant by itself. It's between body and body. The future is between the past and past. Sitting on a chair with a table in between, a body sees a body. The scent of the future is talking to me.

## Ellipsis

With every step a new scene emerges
Footprints keep ahead of the steps

We always hang around at the beginning of a
sentence
like people who have something to say

Birds flying over from beyond the horizon

An airplane that takes off again from where it
landed
A ship that departs again from where it
moored
The waves fight back against the ship; the

atmosphere acrobats away from the plane

Touch my face, my face is sticking out there

My face is the face you touch
I think my face that I'm touching will look sad

On your face is the Big Dipper made up of
seven holes

A sentence that breaks apart every time we step
away

The birds flying over the horizon go over the

curved surface of the Earth;
  silence leads the birds over the horizon


  We'll meet someday


  Touch my eyes
  It's quite spacious inside the brackets

## The Longing Meadow

A hill lush with green
I was looking for something
I think someone told me something important

Thinking about the things I can have
and about the things I can't

How can I tear off the memories that are
stuck?
 the trampled fruits on the soles of my feet?

Shoes that I left in the forest
after cutting the laces that couldn't be untied
A sense of direction that only knows that I'll

go up

One day, I had a dream that I couldn't help but be enthralled by
About things that are so close but ungraspable
About talking about the things that slipped through my hands

I get out of there and walk through a meadow
A face deep in thought
as I tread on the uses of plants that the hills may hold
A face that looks at my face deep in thought

Within me, where even the dying fire revives
with a single gust of wind,
　the person who kept dying died perfectly

# I Have Kept the Faith*

Let's meet in front of the gods. If you pull the trigger, screams pour out before gunfire. A forest where birds fly when you and I fairly share life and death. You who continue to revive from the leaves fluttering from the gunshots. In the forest where laughter and tears echo together, not a drop of blood flows indifferently. The trees shake and dig their roots deeper. I think of you after shooting the past—with a view full of blood. I think about shaking myself even when I'm dead. Like the forest rearing the trees and the trees raising the forest, raising a forest is neither a scream nor a gunshot, but the sound of my breath. You die for eternity as long as I breathe—in a forest where sin is loaded with green. When the days of putting a gun into my mouth become frequent, let's meet in front of the gods.

* 2 Timothy 4:7

## Summer, Decline and Then Blackout

How would it have been if I came a little earlier? I wish I had known this place sooner. A fly flies over a sandwich with only a corner left and we wave it away. Water droplets on the glass fall down to the table and outside is sweltering heat and downpour.

Broken pavements and tables with wobbly legs intertwine regardless of their chronological order. You can think as you please, but everywhere eventually leads to you since our hearts are tied together. Being and the possibility of being lead to us.

When I ask about the title of a song that's playing, you won't say anything; because you're not a person who pretends to know something that you don't.

Let's just live without knowing what we don't know.

Let's not try to know something that we don't.

Let's keep writing; because you're a good person.

Because you're someone who says things like this without blinking an eye

Why do we count heads when we count

people?

Why do we only remember that one look when people have two eyes?

People drinking, talking, laughing, and chatting—it all seems like an act. Our tears and silence must seem like an act from their perspective. Days of sweltering heat and downpour when I didn't dare to go home as the skies poured noise without hesitation.

Even if we leave the city, people live here, and love lives here, and afraid that if we let it out of our mouths it would become word and flee, we sit still in a chair and wave away the fly that's flying back and forth.

We repeatedly lived in such a world—even though there was no one else.

# POET'S NOTE

POET

You force me to choose.
Though you haven't done a thing for me,
you smile with your hands open in front of my
eyes;

I gladly
strike both your hands, turn my back, and
walk away.

No one knows
how many times this sequence happened;

and the result is that I grab a pen and write.
This is what I jot down in a notebook:

Orenadu is steadily being built.
Somewhere in the future,
even though no one's looking for it

# POET'S ESSAY

This trip was relatively short. That's what you think as you exit the last world. Even though it was a short trip, you visited many places and passed by many people. A person walking on a trail with paper cups in both hands. A person riding a bicycle on the riverside and a person who dreams of dreams and a person who repeatedly dreams the same dream. You shared a portion of the story with them.

You open a bag. There are pieces of a bowl, pieces of a sandwich, shiny pieces and so forth rolling around inside. The person obsessing over the birds was really weird. That's what you think as you caress the pieces of a feather.

At first, you intended to keep your distance from them. Like a shadow, you tried to play the role of a signpost to guide them. But a Sherpa is bound to eventually become a companion.

Before you knew it, you found yourself patting someone on the shoulder, riding a bike together, and even making a lunch appointment with someone. On second thought, you behaved as if you were familiar with them from the beginning. The more you spent time with them, the more they felt like your own body, and their circumstances and personalities helplessly invaded you.

In the process of meeting numerous people, you were sometimes confused about your identity, but you felt that it was actually thickening your existence. Your ego came apart and became clear, it divided and scattered far and wide. It was a strange feeling. And soon you wonder if they are not, in fact, you yourself.

You are not who you used to be now. No, the words before and after are no longer needed.

Also, you think that the being that other yous are looking for is also ultimately you yourself. And it hits you—that in the end, every story is connected.

But you're not the talkative type. You're the type that keeps to yourself what you want to say. You're the type that keep to yourself what you want to say and burst out with words that you don't have to.

"      "

When words burst out of your mouth, the story prepares to start again.

# COMMENTARY

POET

# A Monologue to Cross the Space "Between"

Choi Jin Seok (Literary Critic)

## 1. The Empty Place of a Monologue

If you happen to have picked up this poetry collection, you must now choose: to open the book to the first page or to leave it on the table. That choice will soon lead to another choice: to move on to the second page or to close the page as is. I'm not trying to repeat the cliché, "Life is a series of choices." Choices pose significant questions to us. To open to the first page, to put down the book, to turn the second page, or to quit... Two realities that cannot exist at the same time because they cannot be chosen at the same time, questions that face the space "between".

What is clear among the countless options is that just as with the choices we make, we have no idea what consequences an act of unselected moments would have brought. What is clear, however, is that we must take responsibility for them. We must accept and acknowledge the consequences that despite originating in chance, have inevitably reached us. The possibility of infinite choices is stated to be a blessing of free will, but isn't "choice" just rhetoric for inevitable fate? It's an excuse designed to endure the inevitability you face here and now. The fate of the poem is probably no different—the intersection and turning point between the two realities, the tedious and harsh monologue of a poet trapped in the space "between".

The space "between" that connects choice to choice is an empty place where two separate realities meet and separate. Debating whether to write a sentence or not, the poet stays in the space-time of that moment and unravels his story. Although the two possibilities cannot be realized at the same time, they coexist in his story. Simultaneity contains the two faces of impossible reality; just like a face may beam a bright smile or shed sad tears but cannot have the two face each other. So, what is the poet writing about?

## 2. Memory of Eternity

On a table is an empty dish
A dish reflecting a face
What does an empty dish want to hold?

I put it face down on a dish rack
The face reflected on the dish changes ("Dish
Filling", 1-5)

As a daily tableware, a dish is simply a tool
for holding food. However, whenever a face
is reflected on the surface of a dish and looks
different each time, the dish stops being a simple
tool. The dish not only reflects our daily life,
but also captures moments of difference that
we don't recognize day to day. Unfortunately,
we are blind and deaf to the truth reflected on

the dish that we use every day. In the lines that follow, the person who was eating together says that the speaker has changed, but the speaker insists that he is no different from before. The space between them doesn't narrow. Neither of them, at least from their own perspective, will know the truth. Just like that, time passes and they only move further away from each other. If there's something the empty dish really wants to hold, it will be a story that explains this chasm, this invisible space "between" us.

If I close my eyes
a distant memory draws back

Between embarrassment and love
Between countless strolls and humiliation
Between misery and remorse

How much more light can you give me?

Even if that can't burn a clump of grass

an instant is soon an eternity ("I Have Finished the
Race", 11-18)

Engraved in the space "between" is a complex
emotional movement of "embarrassment" and
"love", "stroll" and "humiliation", and "misery"
and "remorse". The choices that come to mind
through the "distant memory"—the movement
of that time between "you" and "I"—are not
objective distances but emotional relationships
formed through the tensions of feelings.
Scenes from memories that have to be watched
from afar like the "eternity" because they are
impossible to measure. If another choice was
possible from the countless space "between",

would we be living a different life from the one right now? "A lot of things happened and a lot of things didn't. … A few memories of hopes and expectations are stored away. They are haunted by a few regrets and despair." ("Planned Community")

### 3. A Secret Song

Being "empty" is not a state of nothingness but a place for an event that has not yet arrived. Likewise, the space "between" is not nonexistence but a place left for something that will exist; here and there, this and that, the ignition points of events that will connect "you" and "I". Whatever that is exactly, it is our responsibility to continue the choices of the "between" again.

I think there is something between us. With those words your body appears in front of me. When I whisper, I love you, I love you, I love you, you become a piece of meat. I think of everything there is to about meat. The more I bite off a thought the harder flesh becomes. The floor, the ceiling, the wall, your face permeates them all. Then you disappear. A thought is fragrant by itself. It's between body and body. The future is between the past and past. Sitting on a chair with a table in between, a body sees a body. The scent of the future is talking to me. ("Sandwich")

Everything is always-already a choice and an action. Feeling and thinking, seeing and talking, being shaken by daydreams... My face reflected on the everyday objects is the expression of the spaces "between" overlapping thoughts of the past and memories of the future, and your "present" reflected in my eyes. We are changing and calling for each other as we move apart without even realizing it. Although "The path that went downhill / and the path that went uphill" gets mixed up and we each decide on the path we will take, "We each took paper cups, saying that the first person to arrive should get the water" ("Walking Trail"). There's no way to tell if this promise will be fulfilled. However, the consecutive choices of walking forward might lead us to "the ground forming" without "here and there", where one "Can't distinguish up from down" ("Synchronicity"). Isn't "between" simply the name of the time and place to discover and invent through the countless formation of choices? Thus, I can only say that the poet's monologue about the impossible reality of simultaneity, where "you" and "I" will discover and invent each other, is a secret song engraved with transparent ink.

I'll tell you the things you'll have to go through from now on

The eyes of a person putting their hand on your shoulder
The rippling past

Some day in the future, I described that as love's advent ("Synchronicity", 19-23)

Synchronicity. This word that contains the paradox of "and/or" brings to mind the Russian word "sobytie" that means to "co-be", co(so) + be(bytie). Often used to indicate an "event", this word suggests that different things that exist together will inevitably generate something else. Whether that something is good or bad, will lead to another meeting place, or will split and spread out, continuing for eternity, no one knows. This is nothing to be happy, sad, or angry about. As beings that exist through these events, it is enough for us to faithfully take responsibility for the "between" of here and now. That's the only reason why "love's advent", or the story of poetry, needs to be filled.

# PRAISE FOR
# LEE JONGMIN

What can we call Lee JongMin's love? A love that is only achieved through relationships with others regardless of external conditions? I want to call it an "unconditional love". It may be possible to criticize the poetic world of Lee JeongMin that progresses little by little through unconditional love for being somewhat romantic and sentimental. This is because reality is different from what "I" is seeking. However, we can think about it this way: only when one clearly sees a romantic worldview different from reality can one begin to think about the blanks left by the space of love that Lee JongMin displays.

Jin Gi-hwan, "The Path of Unconditional Love."
*Paran*, Winter, 2022.

Lee JongMin started his career as a poet by winning the 2015 Munhaksasang New Poet Award in 2015. Since his debut, he has shown a keen interest in marginalized objects and conditions of life, and has devoted himself in discovering the meaning and values of overlooked beings through his poems. The poems in this collection are also trying to find the meaning and value of marginalized and mundane events in life and give form to them.

(...)

By writing down the fragments of life that approach at random, i.e., by writing down events in life based on chance, Lee JeongMin tries to record life as a passive recorder. Such a poetic form, one that focuses on random events and passively records life, could have always been the way to capture the greatness and

wonder of the small and insignificant things in
our daily life.

Hwang Chi-bok, "Various Forms to Capture Life."
*Yeollin Sihak*, Winter, 2018.

K-POET
**Synchronicity**


**Written by** Lee JongMin
**Translated by** Levi Lee
**Published by** ASIA Publishers
**Address** 445, Hoedong-gil, Paju-si, Gyeonggi-do, Korea
(Seoul Office: 161-1, Seodal-ro, Dongjak-gu,Seoul, Korea)
**Email** bookasia@hanmail.net
**ISBN** 979-11-5662-317-5 (set) | 979-11-5662-699-2 (04810)
First published in Korea by ASIA Publishers 2024


*This book is published with the support of the Literature Translation Institute of Korea
(LTI Korea).

# Through literature, you
bilingual Edition Modern

## ASIA Publishers' carefully selected

### Set 1

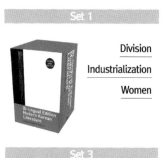

Division

Industrialization

Women

### Set 2

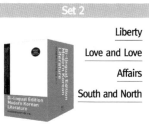

Liberty

Love and Love

Affairs

South and North

### Set 3

Seoul

Tradition

Avant-Garde

### Set 4

Diaspora

Family

Humor

Search "bilingual edition

# can meet the real Korea!
## Korean Literature

## 22 keywords to understand Korean literature

### Set 5

Relationships

Discovering

Everyday Life

Taboo and Desire

### Set 6

Fate

Aesthetic Priests

The Naked in the

Colony

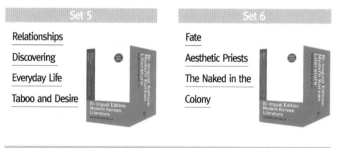

### Set 7

Colonial Intellectuals Turned "Idiots"

Traditional Korea's Lost Faces

Before and After Liberation

Korea After the Korean War

## korean literature"on Amazon!

## K-픽션 시리즈 | Korean Fiction Series

〈K-픽션〉 시리즈는 한국문학의 젊은 상상력입니다. 최근 발표된 가장 우수하고 흥미로운 작품을 엄선하여 출간하는 〈K-픽션〉은 한국문학의 생생한 현장을 국내외 독자들과 실시간으로 공유하고자 기획되었습니다. 〈바이링궐 에디션 한국 대표 소설〉 시리즈를 통해 검증된 탁월한 번역진이 참여하여 원작의 재미와 품격을 최대한 살린 〈K-픽션〉 시리즈는 매 계절마다 새로운 작품을 선보입니다.

001 버핏과의 저녁 식사-**박민규** Dinner with Buffett-**Park Min-gyu**

002 아르판-**박형서** Arpan-**Park hyoung su**

003 애드벌룬-**손보미** Hot Air Balloon-**Son Bo-mi**

004 나의 클린트 이스트우드-**오한기** My Clint Eastwood-**Oh Han-ki**

005 이베리아의 전갈-**최민우** Dishonored-**Choi Min-woo**

006 양의 미래-**황정은** Kong's Garden-**Hwang Jung-eun**

007 대니-**윤이형** Danny-**Yun I-hyeong**

008 퇴근-**천명관** Homecoming-**Cheon Myeong-kwan**

009 옥화-**금희** Ok-hwa-**Geum Hee**

010 시차-**백수린** Time Difference-**Baik Sou linne**

011 올드 맨 리버-**이장욱** Old Man River-**Lee Jang-wook**

012 권순찬과 착한 사람들-**이기호** Kwon Sun-chan and Nice People-**Lee Ki-ho**

013 알바생 자르기-**장강명** Fired-**Chang Kang-myoung**

014 어디로 가고 싶으신가요-**김애란** Where Would You Like To Go?-**Kim Ae-ran**

015 세상에서 가장 비싼 소설-**김민정** The World's Most Expensive Novel-**Kim Min-jung**

016 체스의 모든 것-**김금희** Everything About Chess-**Kim Keum-hee**

017 할로윈-**정한아** Halloween-**Chung Han-ah**

018 그 여름-**최은영** The Summer-**Choi Eunyoung**

019 어느 피씨주의자의 종생기-**구병모** The Story of P.C.-**Gu Byeong-mo**

020 모르는 영역-**권여선** An Unknown Realm-**Kwon Yeo-sun**

021 4월의 눈-**손원평** April Snow-**Sohn Won-pyung**

022 서우-**강화길** Seo-u-**Kang Hwa-gil**

023 가출-**조남주** Run Away-**Cho Nam-joo**

024 연애의 감정학-**백영옥** How to Break Up Like a Winner-**Baek Young-ok**

025 창모-**우다영** Chang-mo-**Woo Da-young**

026 검은 방-**정지아** The Black Room-**Jeong Ji-a**

027 도쿄의 마야-**장류진** Maya in Tokyo-**Jang Ryu-jin**

028 홀리데이 홈-**편혜영** Holiday Home-**Pyun Hye-young**

029 해피 투게더-**서장원** Happy Together-**Seo Jang-won**

030 골드러시-**서수진** Gold Rush-**Seo Su-jin**

031 당신이 보고 싶어하는 세상-**장강명** The World You Want to See-**Chang Kang-myoung**

032 지난밤 내 꿈에-**정한아** Last Night, In My Dream-**Chung Han-ah**

Special 휴가중인 시체-**김중혁** Corpse on Vacation-**Kim Jung-hyuk**

Special 사파에서-**방현석** Love in Sa Pa-**Bang Hyeon-seok**